BLOSSOM

A Girl's Adventures
in Revolutionary Rockland

BLOSSOM

A Girl's Adventures
in Revolutionary Rockland

Eileen Switzer-Clarke

Illustrated by Barbara Janik Carney

The Historical Society of Rockland County

The Historical Society of Rockland County
20 Zukor Road, New City, New York 10956

© 1997 by The Historical Society of Rockland County

Edited by Marjorie H. Bauer
Designed by Paul W. Melone

Funded by Rockland Bicentennial 1998, Inc.

First Edition

Printed in the United States of America by Tech Repro, Inc.

Library of Congress Cataloging-in-Publication Data

Switzer-Clarke, Eileen, 1939-
    Blossom, a girl's adventures in revolutionary Rockland / by Eileen
Switzer-Clarke: [illustrated by Barbara Janik Carney].—1st ed.
        p. cm.
    Summary: When sold in the 1770s to a farmer whose daughter is also
nine-years-old, Blossom proves her mettle in an encounter with
marauding British soldiers during the American Revolution.
    ISBN 0-911183-44-2 (pbk.)

    1. United States—History-Revolution, 1775-1783—Juvenile fiction.

[1. United States—History-Revolution, 1775-1783—Fiction.

2. Slavery—Fiction. 3. Afro-Americans—Fiction.]

I. Carney, Barbara Janik, ill.   II. Title

PZ7.S9825B1   1997

[Fic]—dc21   97-25680

To the schoolchildren of Rockland County
E.S.C.

To my parents, Darius and Dunia Janik
B.J.C.

Author's Acknowledgment

I would like to express my thanks to the people who assisted me in the preparation of this manuscript.

First, to my loving family members for their patience and encouragement. Next, to Marjorie Bauer, not only for her work as editor, but for her buoyant enthusiasm for the work. Last, a special thanks to John Scott of the Historical Society of Rockland County. Without his interest this book would not be possible.

To the Reader:

The story on the following pages is about a girl I've named Blossom. Although her story is fiction, some of the people and events in the story are real. It may be helpful to know about them before you begin reading.

Slavery was legal in Colonial New York. In 1798, a law was passed that freed slaves in stages according to age. The last slaves were freed in 1828. It is important to know this because Blossom is a slave. Her masters own a farm near Quashpeck Pond in Orange County. Over the years, the names of these places have been changed. If you go there today, you'll find yourself at Rockland Lake in Rockland County.

Little Rockland was once part of Orange County. The county was large and travel in Colonial days was difficult. So in 1798, the corner of Orange that was then known as "Orange, South of the Mountains" was formed into a new county named Rockland.

George Washington came to Orange County many times, and since the county government met at Tappan, he visited there too. In the story,

Blossom attends the Dutch Reformed Church in Tappan. The Dutch Reformed Church is still there, although the old building Blossom would have attended has been torn down. A new building was constructed on that site in 1835. Close to the church is a graveyard where both white and black parishioners were buried. If you search carefully, you'll find the grave of at least one slave. Look for the words "the estate of" on a headstone. These words were commonly used to show that the deceased was the property of someone else.

While at church, Blossom sees Dominie Lansing. Reverend Nicholas Lansing did serve at the church, but not during the Revolutionary War. He arrived there in 1784. I've chosen to move the good reverend up in time because he was such an interesting person. He served the church and community for 51 years, from 1784-1835. I've tried to describe him as he really was.

Another real Rockland person is the Indian, Camboan. He once lived somewhere in Upper Nyack, although no one knows exactly when. Legend has it that a local family once asked him to find two little girls lost in the woods.

Camboan was probably a Munsee Indian, one of a group of Indians who, in earlier days, visited Nyack's shores to fish for oysters. The first Indians to settle there probably arrived around 1670. For many years, the ghost of Camboan was thought to haunt the area the Dutch called Verdrietige Hook. Today, that place is part of Hook Mountain State Park.

The calf, Rembrandt, is borrowed from a tale about a real calf owned by Garret Meyer, who lived near Quashpeck Pond. The real calf ran to a tree where Meyer was hiding, thus causing his discovery and capture by British raiders.

Yes, the British did raid farms in Rockland. In Nyack, a group of men formed a militia to protect themselves from attack by British ships that came up the Hudson River. These militiamen called themselves the "River Guard."

One of the warships was named *Vulture.* It was that ship that brought Major André to Haverstraw to receive maps of the West Point fortifications from Benedict Arnold. The last British warship to come up the Hudson was

Perseverance. In 1783, it anchored off Sparkill while Sir Guy Carleton met with George Washington to iron out plans for the British evacuation of our new nation.

Blossom never met George Washington, but she does help to defeat the enemy. I hope you will enjoy reading about her and come to like her as much as I have liked writing about her.

The Storyteller

CONTENTS

THE SALE

Blossom sat dangling her feet from the end of the wagon as it bumped along King's Highway. It was hot, even for July, but Blossom didn't notice the heat. She was remembering the whispered voices older black people used when they talked about slave sales. She wished she'd paid more attention to what they'd said, but she hadn't. One thing was plain though: a sale was something every slave feared. Now it was happening to her, and she didn't understand why.

"They must be punishing me for something, but I know I never did anything bad," she said to herself. "I did all my chores. Mistress Braun would have switched me good if I didn't do just what she said. She likes being mean and this is her meanest ever."

Her master, Jacob Braun, sat at the front of the wagon. "Get along there, Shotzie," he called to his horse. "There's money up ahead, and I aim to have it before dark."

Old Braun was never in a good mood unless there was money to be made. Today, he was unusally happy.

"Shotzie," he boasted, "we're on our way to meet a fool. His name's Jarvis VanEyck and he's going to give me one hundred and thirty dollars for Blossom. She's not worth it, I say. Now her mother was different. That woman was worth every penny I paid."

Just then, the wagon wheel struck a stone and bounced Blossom up from the buckboard. The burlap sack next to her flew into the air, too. All her clothes were in that sack and she didn't want to lose it. What if the new masters gave her nothing to wear? She lunged and caught the sack before it could tumble into the road.

Mr. Braun took no notice of Blossom. He was still busy telling his horse about her mother. "It was a bad luck day when that woman died and left me this useless child to feed."

Blossom could hear old Braun, and she wondered if he was selling her because she ate too much. It was certainly true that she was always hungry, but she couldn't help it with the stingy portions Mistress Braun put on her plate.

At a crossroads Mr. Braun turned the horse and headed east. "We'll be there soon," he called over his shoulder.

Blossom felt her knees shake and her hands get sweaty.

"And, Blossom," Mr. Braun went on, "you act real sweet with these folks. VanEyck's got a daughter your age. He wants you to keep her company and I don't want him thinking you're unfit for his girl."

Blossom's hands were getting wetter. She wiped them against the coarse sack, but it didn't do any good.

The wagon finally came to a stop in front of a stone farmhouse. A tall man stood in the doorway. He waved a greeting to Mr. Braun, then invited him inside. Blossom climbed down from the buckboard and followed.

The men went into the parlor. Blossom stood in the doorway. She watched as the new man took two clay pipes and tobacco from the mantel. For a while, he and Mr. Braun puffed and chatted in Dutch. Lots of Colonial New Yorkers spoke Dutch, especially when there was news about the war or George Washington.

Soon Mr. Braun took some papers from his pocket and read aloud, this time in English.

"I, Jacob Braun," he began, "hereby sell one African slave named Blossom to Jarvis VanEyck. I also make it known that this slave is nine years of age, simple of mind, and is without any skill or talent."

He went on reading, but Blossom no longer wanted to listen. She hated Mr. Braun, she hated his words and

6

she hated having to stand there while two white men talked about her.

She looked around the room. Brightly colored curtains trimmed the windows and gaily painted Dutch shoes were set on the sills. Near the fireplace a cuddly rag doll sat in a rocking chair. It had brown wool hair, and blue X's had been sewn on as eyes.

The men were still talking and Blossom saw the new man take gold coins from a pouch he held. She pretended the men weren't there and turned to face the soft doll.

Soon the men got to their feet. Mr. Braun patted the gold in his pocket and said, "She's yours now, Jarvis, and I think you'll regret having her."

Then stepping closer to Blossom, he whispered, "If you know what's good for you, you'll be real nice to his girl."

The rag doll was watching and suddenly Blossom hated it too.

When Mr. Braun was gone, the new man led Blossom into the kitchen where Mrs. VanEyck waited with her daughter.

Blossom didn't look at them. She kept her eyes on the floor. The only things she saw were shoes and even they made her feel ashamed. The girl's shoes were soft and new. Her own shoes had once belonged to Mrs. Braun. They were too big and had cracks in the leather.

The new mistress explained all the jobs Blossom was to do. She guided her through the house, out to the well, the barn and even to the vegetable garden.

When they were back in the kitchen Mrs. VanEyck gave Blossom a cup of cool buttermilk and a slice of bread. While she ate, the girl kept staring, but Blossom refused to look back.

Then, as it was growing late, Mrs. VanEyck took hold of Blossom's clothing sack and led the way up a narrow staircase to the attic where Blossom would sleep.

Blossom looked around. There was a cot and a night stand by the window. The rest of the attic was filled with household items stored in boxes and barrels. She was glad when Mrs. VanEyck left, but the light of her candle cast unfriendly shadows all around her. Blossom placed the candle on the night stand and picked up a piece of broken mirror.

She studied her face carefully. It was a nice face, she thought. She liked her large brown eyes and dark lashes. She liked her full lips and flat nose. She guessed the girl downstairs must have an ugly pointed nose. Thinking that, Blossom pinched her nostrils together and stuck her tongue out at the face in the mirror. Next, she looked at her hair.

When she was younger, Blossom's mother had kept her hair in four pigtails. Every week her mother undid

the braids and washed her hair. Then she rebraided it, tying each pigtail with a strand of colored yarn. Blossom loved the pigtails and the colored yarn.

After her mother died, Mrs. Braun took up the job of washing Blossom's hair. The first time she did it, Mrs. Braun tried to comb out the hair with a fine wooden comb, but the comb broke in the thick curls. That made Mrs. Braun so angry she took a scissors and cut off all of Blossom's hair.

Now, standing in the attic, Blossom brushed her hand over her head and put down the mirror. She wondered why God hadn't made everyone the same color, but she didn't know the answer to that.

She blew out the candle, and without undressing, she laid down on the cot. It was dark. For the first time all day, Blossom let hot tears flow down her cheeks.

THE NEW HOME

Blossom thought her first week at the VanEyck home went well. The new mistress seemed nice. At least she didn't yell the way old Mistress Braun had done. Sure, Blossom still had lots of jobs to do, but most of them were finished by noontime. The rest of the day she played with the girl. Her name was Eloise.

The problem with Eloise was that she thought she was someone special. Her mother dressed her in pretty dresses with tulips stitched on them. Her father called her his "golden-haired beauty." Worst of all, Eloise was always the boss and Blossom always had to obey her.

When they played on the swing that Mr. VanEyck had made for Eloise, it was Blossom's job to push to get Eloise started. Then Blossom had to watch Eloise's blond curls flop up and down while Eloise had fun on the swing. When Eloise tired of the swing, Blossom got to take a turn. Just when Blossom got the swing going

12

really high, Eloise would say Blossom's turn was over.

When they went to the barn to jump in the hay, Eloise made Blossom go first to check for spider webs. If Eloise even saw a spider, the game was over. That was another thing about Eloise Blossom didn't like—Eloise was a coward. Anything that crawled made her squeal.

One day they went fishing. Eloise made Blossom dig up the worms they needed. Of course, Eloise hid her eyes while Blossom put a worm on the fishhook. Then, when everything was ready, Eloise got to do the fishing. She stood daintily on the rock by the creek, so as not to get her new shoes wet, and waited for a fish to nibble at the bait.

After a short while she said, "This game isn't any fun. The fish don't want to bite my hook. Come on, Blossom, let's go play with my doll."

When she stepped carefully from the rock onto the dry shore, Blossom pleaded, "Miss Eloise, can I have a try? Maybe I'll catch one."

Eloise had already started for the house. She called over her shoulder, "Blossom, if the fish won't bite when I hold the pole, they won't bite when you hold it either. We're going to play with my doll. She always does just what I want her to do."

Each evening, after Blossom helped Mrs. VanEyck clean the dinner dishes, Mr. VanEyck called the girls

13

together for Bible lessons. He began by reading a passage, then asked questions to test their knowledge.

No matter how many answers Blossom got right, Mr. VanEyck never praised her. But if Eloise knew even one answer, her father beamed and said something dumb like, "My clever little angel." Finally, Bible lessons ended with Eloise reading a psalm. No one had ever bothered to teach Blossom to read, so listening to Eloise made her feel unimportant.

Blossom didn't like Bible lessons, but what happened next made up for it.

Just before bedtime, Mrs. VanEyck combed Eloise's blond hair and twisted it around strips of cloth to make her long curls. It was Blossom's job to hand Mrs. VanEyck the cloth strips she used. Blossom would stand by waiting for the comb to get caught in a tangle and make Eloise yelp. Blossom never thought a white girl could have so many tangles.

No matter how much Eloise squirmed or cried, Mrs. VanEyck just kept on combing. Each and every curl got the same treatment.

When Blossom handed over the last cloth strip and it was time to head up the narrow staircase for bed, she always glanced back for one last look at Eloise's red puffy eyes. Then she skipped up the stairs with a smile.

14

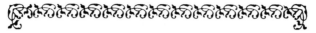

THE PRANK

On Sunday morning, Blossom awoke and dressed hurriedly. Breakfast would be very simple this morning. Every Sunday while the weather was good, the VanEycks went to the Dutch church in the village of Tappan.

Blossom washed her face at the well and carried a bucket of water into the kitchen. Mrs. VanEyck was warming day-old biscuits at the fire. She called, "Blossom, see if Eloise needs help getting ready."

Eloise was in the parlor where a fancy copper tray was hung on the wall. She was wearing a new pink dress and was looking at her reflection in the shiny metal.

"Blossom, do these buttons for me," Eloise ordered.

While Blossom worked at the little buttons, Eloise asked, "Isn't this the prettiest dress ever?"

In her mind, Blossom had to agree that the dress was very pretty, but she couldn't bring herself to tell that to Eloise. She searched her mind for something else to say and finally settled on, "Your mama did a fine job sewing it."

"I think I'm going to look wonderful today," Eloise boasted. "People hardly ever see you except in church. That's why you get dressed up when you go there."

Eloise was being prideful and Blossom wanted her to know it.

"Miss Eloise, you'd better not let your mama hear you. She don't want you going to church to show off, she wants you to go there to pray."

"I will!" snapped Eloise. Then, placing her hands on her hips, she glared at Blossom and said, "You're just jealous 'cause nobody's going to look at you."

Blossom wanted to grab the yellow curls and yank them, not because she was jealous, but because what Eloise had just said was true. No one was going to look at her—no one ever did.

Blossom turned angrily on her heel and went back into the kitchen to help Mrs. VanEyck.

Later, when her chores were done, she sat on the front steps and waited for the family to start out for church. While she waited, she straightened her collar. She checked that her hands were clean, then used the hem of her skirt to shine her shoes.

From inside the house came the sound of Mrs. VanEyck humming. It reminded Blossom of her mother. She wished her mother was with her today.

16

Mr. VanEyck led the horse and wagon into the front yard and called to his wife to hurry. "Maria, what's keeping you?"

Mrs. VanEyck answered from the window. "Just a little longer. We're almost ready."

It was about this time that Blossom noticed a grasshopper stretched out on a rhododendron leaf close by. "Hello there," she said and waved her pointer finger in greeting.

The grasshopper paid no notice. He went on sunning himself.

"Eloise, put on your bonnet. A proper lady never gets sun on her face," Blossom heard Mrs. VanEyck say.

"But, Mother," Eloise protested, "the bonnet crushes my curls."

Mrs. VanEyck's voice took on a firmer tone. "Do as you're told, Eloise. I won't have you covered with freckles."

"I don't care," Eloise said stubbornly. "I hate that old thing."

Soon the door opened and Mrs. VanEyck stepped into the yard. Eloise walked behind her wearing a bonnet. They headed for the wagon and were climbing aboard when Mrs. VanEyck remembered something.

"Blossom, hurry and fetch the drawstring purse I made to go with Eloise's dress."

17

Blossom ran toward the house. As she neared the steps, she noticed the grasshopper still sitting on the rhododendron bush. She bent forward and scooped it up. She had an idea!

In the bedroom, she found the pink purse. She opened it and pushed the grasshopper inside. Then quickly she pulled the drawstrings tight.

When they arrived at church, Blossom went to a place close behind the building where a row of small gravestones had been set off from the others. She stopped in front of the newest stone. Although she couldn't read, she knew what was written there.

Dinnah
Property of Jacob Braun

"Hello, Mama," she thought, looking at the stone. "I know you watch over me, so I try to do things just like you taught me."

Then, looking around to be sure no one was nearby, she said aloud, "I wish you were here. Nobody likes me the way you did. Master Braun said I was useless. At least, I can do up buttons. A person who can't do buttons is useless, but no one cares about that. No one cares about me."

Briefly she closed her eyes and remembered the warmth of her mother's soft lips against her cheek.

18

Then opening her eyes, she reached out and touched the stone. It was hard and cold.

In the distance, she heard the bustle of people entering the church and Blossom knew it was getting late. "I have to go, Mama," she said. "Have a nice time

in Heaven." She started to leave, then stopped and turned back to the gravestone. "And don't worry," she called. "I'm getting enough to eat now."

With that, she ran to the back door of the church. She went upstairs to the balcony and found a seat with the other black worshipers.

Eloise and her parents went in by the main door.

Blossom watched them take their seats in their family pew. From where she sat, Blossom had a good view of everything and everyone. The only better view was the one Dominie Lansing had from the pulpit.

The dominie was very tall and skinny. He had a long nose with a bump on it. Blossom thought the bump was just perfect for holding his spectacles in place. She also thought he prayed a lot because there were holes in the knees of his breeches.

He knew everyone's secrets and often told them in church. His bony finger would reach over the pulpit while his deep scolding voice said, "The Lord knows you haven't given to charity, Jan Clausen," or some other horrid thing.

The dominie began with a scripture reading, then shifted to a long sermon in Dutch. Blossom didn't understand any of what he said but she tried not to fidget. She also tried to keep an eye on Eloise.

Eloise had slipped off her bonnet so her pretty hair could be seen. Other than that, Eloise was playing the perfect little girl.

Blossom had given up hope of anything interesting happening in Eloise's corner when she heard Dominie Lansing's strong voice say, "Servants, obey your masters."

That was how he always started the special sermon he preached to the black people. Blossom had to shift her eyes to the pulpit, so she didn't see Eloise fussing with the strings of her tiny purse.

Everyone was silent. Dominie Lansing explained that this morning he would read about the people Jesus called "Blessed." Blossom had heard about the Blesseds before. She took a deep breath and settled back in her seat to prepare for the list of the Blesseds to come.

Just then the peaceful little church was blasted by a piercing "Oooooooie!" Every eye turned to the VanEyck family pew. Even the good preacher stopped speaking to gape in disbelief at the source of the loud noise.

There was Eloise hopping up and down, swatting wildly at her curls, repeating, "Ooooooooie! Ooooooooie!" with the most improper, unladylike howl ever heard in the little Dutch church.

Thanks to Eloise, Dominie Lansing skipped all the Blesseds that morning except for one Blossom had never heard before. "Blessed are the silent," he said.

Blossom sang the final hymn with a loud and happy voice. She was sure Jesus had gained a new Blessed for his list, and it was hard to keep from laughing each time she looked at Eloise's messy hair.

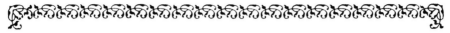

STRANGER IN THE BARN

On Monday, a team of oxen stopped at the farm. The driver was Garret Blauvelt. He was hauling stone from a nearby quarry.

"Hello, Jarvis," Garret called in a friendly voice.

Mr. VanEyck put aside a broken shutter he was repairing and went to greet him.

"I'm glad to have your company, Garret. Come inside for something cool to drink," he said.

"Thank you, neighbor, but I don't dare," the older man said in a serious tone. Climbing down from his wagon he stepped closer to Mr. VanEyck and lowered his voice.

"There's bad news. An English warship is anchored in the Hudson River. It's named the *Vulture* and it's not four miles from here."

He paused to allow Mr. VanEyck to realize the full danger of the situation. Then he said, "Last night, men from the ship went into Haverstraw. Two of the townspeople were murdered. Three homes were burned. And, damn them, the *Vulture* is still out in the river."

Jarvis VanEyck's face grew pale. This kind of thing had happened before. The English needed food for their army and they got it by stealing from local families. If the warship stayed in the river it meant there would be another raid.

Jarvis clenched his fists. "Isn't there anything we can do to stop them?"

"We've no cannons, so there's little harm we can do to the ship," Garret Blauvelt answered. "We militiamen must keep our muskets ready. If we catch them on land, we'll give them a fight.

"We've got men watching the river. If they lower small boats into the water, our men will light signal fires along the Palisades. If you see the signals, make haste to Snedecker's Landing. We'll meet there. Hopefully we'll catch the scoundrels and teach them a lesson."

Jarvis VanEyck was resolute. "I'll be ready and I'll be there if I'm needed."

During the days that followed, Mr. VanEyck carried his musket and powder horn with him everywhere he went. The girls were ordered to stay in the house, which they did—except Blossom. She still had to feed the chickens.

Early one morning as she entered the barn, she

24

heard something. She listened again, then shrugged. She found the wooden box that held the chicken feed and began scooping it out.

Suddenly she got the spookiest feeling. Her skin began to tingle and the little hairs on her arms stood up. Silently she closed the feed bin and looked around. The barn was filled with deep shadows—just the thing Blossom hated. She peered into each corner, but nothing was out of place.

Bossie mooed loudly. Matilda answered with a kick to the stall door.

"That's it!" thought Blossom. "Someone's hiding here—the cows are frightened, too!"

She tiptoed out of the barn. Once in the open, she ran as fast as she could to the house.

The VanEyck's were assembled in the kitchen. Mrs. VanEyck was fanning ashes in the fireplace. Eloise was taking plates from the cupboard. Mr. VanEyck, who had overslept, was rubbing the sleep from his eyes. Everyone came to a stop as Blossom flew through the door.

"Someone's hiding in the barn," she blurted out.

Mrs. VanEyck laughed. "There's no one in our barn."

Then, taking Blossom by the shoulders, she turned her to face the door. "Go outside and fetch my eggs," she said firmly.

"Wait!" Mr. VanEyck's strong voice commanded. "Blossom, stay here. I'll go have a look."

No one spoke as Mr. VanEyck took his musket from its rack and left the house.

He returned, with a broad smile on his face. "There's no one there, but soon we'll have a surprise," he laughed. "You girls stay here and tidy up. Mother and I have work to do."

Neither Blossom nor Eloise knew what to make of all that was happening, but they had been told to stay inside and they did. Eloise decided to turn housework into a game. Of course, she played the part of the mother and Blossom played the part of the slave who did all the work.

When Mrs. VanEyck called the girls to come to the barn, they found Mr. VanEyck in a stall with Bossie. At her feet lay a newborn calf.

Bossie lowered her head and breathed in the smell of her baby. She mooed a soft, deep-throated sound. The calf looked at her and answered with a squeak that made Blossom giggle.

Bossie pushed the calf firmly with her nose. The little calf drew its trembling legs under it and tried to stand, but soon toppled into the hay.

"Oh, Father, is something wrong with it?" asked Eloise.

26

"No, Pet," her father reassured her. "It just needs practice working all its legs at the same time."

Bossie stomped the barn floor nervously. Mr. VanEyck stroked her head to quiet her, then pulled her in the direction of the calf again. She licked the moist calf with her strong tongue. "Try again," she seemed to say.

The calf just looked at its mother in bewilderment.

Eloise laughed, "It's saying, 'Leave me alone, Mother Cow.'"

Bossie mooed at her scrawny infant. The calf gave another shrill moo and struggled to its feet. This time Mr. VanEyck was there to put his strong arm under the calf's belly and help it steady itself. When Mr. VanEyck let go, the calf looked at him with grateful brown eyes.

Mr. VanEyck patted Bossie again. Then he tied a rope to her collar and led her out of the barn. When he returned, he used a rag to dry the calf's shaggy white coat.

"It's a girl," he said to Eloise. "You'll have to think of a pretty name for her."

Blossom looked at Eloise's happy face. "Eloise! Eloise! Always Eloise," she thought. Then she stepped back and waited to hear what Eloise would say.

"I think it should be a Dutch name. Everyone will like that," Eloise said.

Blossom rolled her eyes and smirked.

"Rembrandt! Let's call her Rembrandt," Eloise announced.

Mr. and Mrs. VanEyck looked at each other and grinned. Mrs. VanEyck shook her head. "Rembrandt is a man's name. He was an artist in Holland."

"Yes, Mother, I know. He painted pretty pictures, didn't he? I think our calf is pretty enough for an artist to paint. Can't we call her Rembrandt?"

"Well," answered her father, "I suppose she won't mind if we do."

So it was decided.

"Rembrandt," thought Blossom. "I knew she'd pick something dumb!"

For the next few weeks, Rembrandt nursed at Bossie's udder. Then Mr. VanEyck put her in a separate corral and began to feed her grain and milk from a pail. After that, Rembrandt watched for Mr. VanEyck as if he were her mother. And when she was able, which she often was, she got out of the corral to follow him around.

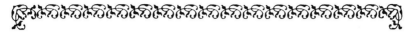

MOSES IN THE BASKET

Later that month, news arrived that the warship had disappeared from the river. Mr. VanEyck put his musket back in its rack by the front door and the girls were again allowed to leave the yard.

The weather was hot, so Eloise planned a picnic near Quashpeck Pond. Her mother prepared a snack and placed it in a little basket with a wooden cover. The girls knew she used the basket to hold sewing threads and needles, so they promised to bring it home safely.

Blossom carried the basket while Eloise led the way through the woods. When they arrived, Blossom saw that Quashpeck Pond wasn't a pond at all. It was a large and deep lake.

Eloise chose a big flat rock at the water's edge as the best place for their picnic. There was an oak tree nearby whose branches provided plenty of shade. From there, the girls could see white water lilies growing in the lake. It was the perfect spot.

They sat on the rock and opened the basket. Inside were four sugar cookies wrapped neatly in a linen towel. There were two cups and a jar with a cork stopper. When they uncapped the jar, they discovered Mrs. VanEyck had prepared a cool berry punch for them to share.

They spread the linen towel out on the rock and placed the picnic things on it. Then they drank punch and ate the delicious cookies.

"Your mama sure makes good cookies, Miss Eloise," Blossom said with her mouth full.

"Of course she does," Eloise said.

Blossom hated when Eloise boasted. "My mama used to make ginger cookies shaped like little Dutch windmills. Can your mama do that, Miss Eloise?"

Eloise stopped chewing. In all the time they'd been together, Eloise had never thought that Blossom might have a mother. She knew her father had bought Blossom, and she was sure her father would never do anything wrong. Still there was something about buying a person that suddenly didn't seem right and it worried her.

"Where is your mother?" she wanted to know.

"In Heaven," Blossom answered softly. Then, seeing Eloise's surprised expression, she added, "Last winter she got a fever. Mistress Braun made herb medicine

32

but it didn't do any good."

Eloise couldn't think of anything worse than not having a mother, so she felt sorry for Blossom. At the same time, she was glad Blossom's mother was dead because she didn't have to worry about owning her.

"Blossom, you're an orphan like Moses in the Bible. He went to live with Pharaoh. You've come to live with us. We'll take care of you from now on," she said as she poured the last of the punch into Blossom's cup.

Blossom knew Eloise never got her Bible stories quite right. "Moses had a mama and a papa, but they had to send him away," she corrected.

Eloise ignored Blossom's words and went on. "Moses went to live with Pharaoh and the kindly princess. That made him an orphan just like you."

"Maybe," Blossom shrugged.

Eloise was full of energy. "Let's play Moses," she cried. "You can be his mother. I'll be Pharaoh's beautiful daughter."

Eloise held up Mrs. VanEyck's basket and continued, "We'll make believe Moses is in this basket. You can float it on the lake, and I can save him."

Blossom smiled. She held up the empty jar. "This can be baby Moses," she said.

She wrapped the jar in the towel as if it were a baby's blanket and cradled it in her arms. Then she

33

bent forward and kissed the jar tenderly.

"Oh, my poor boy," she said dramatically. "I must hide you from the evil soldiers who want to kill you. Don't be scared. Your mama will save you."

With that, she placed baby Moses into the basket and shut the wooden lid.

Eloise was on her feet, giving orders. "You stand on one side of the rock and I'll stand on the other. That's where my palace will be. Then you can put the basket in the lake and push it in my direction."

34

The girls climbed down from the rock and took their positions. Blossom couldn't see Eloise, but she heard her.

"I'm a princess. I'm so beautiful." And Blossom heard Princess Eloise calling to her make-believe servants, "Oh, maids, come and attend me. I'm so beautiful."

Blossom moved closer to the edge of the lake. She opened the basket one more time to look at little Moses.

"You sleep now, baby," she said sweetly. Then she closed the lid and placed the basket in the water. She gave it a shove and waving her arm, she called, "Good-by, big boy!"

Eloise heard Blossom's last words and knew that Moses had been placed in the lake. She waited for the basket to come into view. In a few moments she saw it. But instead of drifting close in to the shoreline, the basket had drifted several feet out into the lake—and it was sinking.

What would her mother say if they came home without the little basket? Without hesitating, Eloise stepped into the water. In only a few steps she would have it. But as she moved forward, she created ripples in the water that pushed the basket even farther away.

Eloise's shoes and long skirt were already wet, so she took three more big steps. Just as she grabbed the basket she felt herself sinking. This was awful! Mud seeped into her shoes. Slimy plants wrapped their long

35

stems around her legs. She fought to move her feet, but the mud held them fast. Finally, she lost her balance and fell over in the water.

"Help! Blossom, help! I'm drowning," she cried in panic.

Just then, Blossom came around the big rock to see Pharaoh's daughter fetch Moses and the basket. Instead of the beautiful princess, she saw Eloise splashing in the mud.

That part of the lake didn't look very deep, so Blossom stepped into the water. With a few strong steps she was at Eloise's side. First she took the basket from Eloise's hand and flung it onto the shore. Next she grabbed Eloise's arms and pulled her to her feet. Soon the two girls walked out of the water together.

"Oh, thank you," Eloise said, as she threw her arms around Blossom and hugged her.

"I didn't do much, Miss Eloise," Blossom explained as she wrestled free of Eloise's muddy arms.

Just as Eloise let go of Blossom, she noticed something odd. "Blossom, your apron pocket is bouncing."

Blossom held open the pocket and looked inside.

"Miss Eloise! Look, I've caught a fish," she said in surprise.

Eloise looked into the pocket. Sure enough, a small minnow was trapped there.

"You're the best fisherman in the world, Blossom," Eloise cried. "You don't even need a fishing pole when you fish."

With that, Eloise threw herself to the ground and laughed. She laughed as she watched Blossom drop the minnow in the lake, and she laughed until she thought of something awful. If a minnow had gotten into Blossom's clothes, maybe something had gotten into her clothes too.

"Blossom, we're going to take off our wet things and shake them out," she ordered. "We can let them dry in the sun."

So the girls took off their shoes and stockings and their skirts and petticoats. They hung them over some bushes. Then, wearing only their undershirts and drawers, they climbed back up on the big rock to wait.

When they were settled side by side and Blossom saw Eloise's pasty white legs next to her own, she was amused. "We sure look different," she laughed.

"Not so different, I guess," Eloise answered thoughtfully.

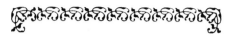

CAMBOAN

When their clothes were dry, Blossom and Eloise put them on and left the lake. They walked back through the woods and were soon on the road that led to the farm. Blossom carried the little basket and swung it as she walked. She was in a happy mood.

"Miss Eloise, your mama's going to ask how our dresses got all wrinkly. What should we tell her?" she asked.

"We'll tell the truth," Eloise answered in her know-it-all way. "I always tell the truth. That's a virtue."

Blossom stopped swinging the basket. She couldn't believe her ears. She'd heard Eloise say some dumb things, but this seemed too dumb even for Eloise. "Are you sure your mama will think it was a virtue to take our clothes off?" she asked.

Eloise gave Blossom's hand a squeeze. "We just won't tell that part," she said with a wide smile. "We'll just say I fell in the lake and you saved me. Mother will like that."

Blossom nodded that she understood. So now they shared a secret. Blossom was delighted. Her toe found a little rock and she gave it a kick. Then Eloise gave it a kick. They were still looking at the rock when a man stepped out of the woods in front of them.

Both girls came to a quick halt! Blossom ducked behind Eloise to hide.

"Sure is an odd-looking fellow," she thought as she peeked over Eloise's shoulder.

The man's skin was darker than any white man's Blossom had seen, yet it was paler than her own. The really odd thing was his hair. One side of the man's head was shaved bald. From the other side hung a long black braid with three brown feathers fixed to the top of it.

"Hey!" the man said in a way that Blossom thought meant "hello," but she wasn't sure. He may have meant "good-by" because no sooner had he spoken than he vanished into the woods.

"Who was that?" Blossom asked from her hiding place.

"That's Camboan," Eloise whispered. "Come on, let's hurry home."

The mood had changed. Eloise wore a frown and was walking briskly. Blossom was so filled with questions, she blurted them all out at one time.

"Why we hurrying, Miss Eloise? Are you afraid of that man? What's the matter with his hair?"

Eloise didn't get a chance to answer. Just then the farmhouse came into view and they saw Rembrandt prancing in the front yard.

Eloise cried out, "Oh, oh! Mother's flower garden!"

Both girls broke into a run yelling, "Rembrandt, no! Rembrandt, no!"

Blossom was the first into the yard. She grabbed the calf's collar and led her away from the garden. It was too late though. Rembrandt had already stepped on some of the bright flowers.

"Poor daisies!" Eloise managed to say as she caught her breath. "Blossom, you take Rembrandt back to the corral. I'll take these inside and put them in a vase."

Blossom tugged gently at Rembrandt's collar, and the white calf, who didn't know she'd done anything wrong, followed happily.

When Blossom got back to the house, she saw a chipped mug full of daisies on the dinner table. Mrs. VanEyck was at the hearth, stirring stew with a big ladle, and Eloise was telling her mother about the picnic.

"And, Mother, that's the truth. If Blossom hadn't been there, I'd of drowned."

Mrs. VanEyck stepped back from the fire. The look

42

on her face was anything but happy. "That lake is dangerous!" she said waving her ladle with each word. "Eloise VanEyck, you should have known better than to go near the water. What ever were you thinking?"

Eloise was shocked. She thought her mother should be delighted with the news that she'd been saved.

"But, Mother," she stammered, "I was trying to get your basket. I know you need it."

Mrs. VanEyck's words took on a softer tone. "I don't need a basket, Eloise. I can always get a new one, but I can't get a new daughter. You must promise never to go near the lake again."

"I promise," Eloise said meekly.

Blossom was now afraid she was next to be yelled at. After all, she was the one who put the basket in the water.

When Mrs. VanEyck turned back to stirring the stew, Blossom breathed a sigh. Stepping closer to Eloise she said, "It's a good thing you didn't tell—you know what."

Eloise let out a giggle.

Mr. VanEyck soon entered the kitchen and they all sat down to their meal. Of course, Mrs. VanEyck told her husband about the basket and how Blossom had dragged Eloise from sure death in the lake.

Mr. VanEyck slammed his hand down loudly on the table.

Instantly, Blossom steeled herself for the blame that was to come.

"That's grand, Blossom!" he said loudly. "I knew you were worth having. I can't wait to see old skinflint Braun's face when I tell him about this."

"Jarvis!" his wife cried. "How can you think of Jacob Braun when Eloise might've drowned?"

"Now, Maria, the lake isn't deep near the shore."

Leaning closer to Blossom, he asked cheerily, "Do you like bread pudding, Blossom?"

Blossom's eyes grew large. "Yes, sir, Master VanEyck. I sure do," she answered.

"Well," confided Mr. VanEyck, "I happen to know your mistress has made bread pudding for dessert. I think you deserve a double helping."

Mrs. VanEyck frowned at her husband, but soon nodded her approval.

With her mother in a good mood again, Eloise relaxed and became her chatty self. "By the way, we met Camboan today."

Instantly, her mother looked displeased again. "That Indian? I hope you didn't speak to him, dear. Why the man is practically a savage."

At the word "Indian" Blossom gulped. "So that's it," she thought. "An Indian. No wonder he looked so strange."

Mr. VanEyck's voice was firm. "Mother, that's not fair. Camboan is a fine neighbor. You say those things only because he looks different."

"Yes, he does look different. If he'd wear his hair like other men I'd feel safer."

"Nonsense," her husband insisted. "Camboan wears his hair that way because he's the last Munsee Indian living in these parts and he's proud of his heritage. There's plenty of other men I trust less."

In her heart Mrs. VanEyck knew her husband was right, so she didn't argue. Instead, she left the table and returned with four bowls of bread pudding.

Blossom's bowl was heaped so high she didn't know where to begin to eat it all. The top seemed as good a place as any. She aimed her spoon and dug in.

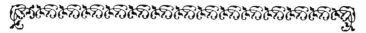

THE INDIAN GAME

The next morning, something in the kitchen smelled good. Blossom didn't know what it was, but she was sure she wanted to eat it. Her mistress was bending near the fire in such a way that Blossom couldn't see what she was making.

As she worked, Mrs. VanEyck told the girls all the chores she wanted done that day. Blossom was to clean the whole parlor, while Eloise got to pick a pot of string beans for dinner.

"Blossom," Mrs. VanEyck said over her shoulder, "when you do the floor, I want you to put sand down and brush it. Then sweep up the sand and wash the floor." Turning away from the fire she approached the table.

Waffles! Blossom was delighted. Mrs. VanEyck had prepared a plate full of waffles.

"Oh, yes," Mrs. VanEyck added. "Eloise, when you finish with the beans, be sure to work on your sampler."

Blossom ate two sweet waffles, then got to work.

47

Cleaning the parlor took time. Mrs. VanEyck liked everything in the room to be perfect, so Blossom was careful to do everything just right. When the floor was spotless, she dusted the table and the mantel. Lastly, she took the candlesticks outside to clean away the wax drippings. When she returned the candlesticks to their place on the mantel, she looked around. Everything was done, so she went outside to find Eloise.

The little seamstress was under a shady tree working on her sampler. Blossom settled herself on the ground nearby.

Eloise was sewing tiny stitches into a square cloth. Someone had drawn letters onto the cloth and Eloise was sewing over them with colored thread.

"Why you doing that?" Blossom asked.

"Because Mother makes me do it. She says every girl has to practice her stitches on a sampler. It's very hard to do, too. If I don't do each letter just right, Mother makes me take the thread out and do the letter all over again. I had to do that one four times."

Blossom looked where Eloise pointed. Stitches in that letter were perfect, but Blossom noticed other letters that made her want to laugh. Of course she didn't. She knew Eloise had tried her best.

"I like the red one," Blossom said. "Red's my

favorite color."

"That's *B*," Eloise said. Then, looking at Blossom, she added, "*B* is for Blossom."

Blossom smiled. Finding a stick, she copied *B* on the ground next to her.

When Eloise saw what Blossom had done, she got an idea. "Blossom, I can use the sampler to teach you to read. See, this is *A*. *A* is for Adam."

Then she made Blossom scratch *A* into the ground with the stick. They did *B, C, D* and all the other letters the same way until they came to the one Eloise was still working on. "This one is *I*," she said. "*I* is for Indian."

Blossom looked at the pink letter. "If *I* is for Indian, you should've used brown thread, Miss Eloise. See, *I* looks like the brown feather the Indian wore."

Suddenly, Eloise jumped to her feet. "Come on, Blossom. I've got a new game." She tugged at Blossom's skirt and added, "We're going to be Indians!"

Blossom got up slowly. The day was hot and she wanted to stay longer under the tree, but Eloise was already marching away.

In the yard they found two chicken feathers. When Blossom slipped one into her hair, her thick curls held the feather in place. Eloise was wearing a bonnet. She knew her mother would be angry if she took it off for long, so she poked a hole in it and pushed the feather through. The feather stood tall at the back of the bonnet.

Blossom laughed. Eloise looked silly. But then, being silly was what made games so much fun.

With their Indian headdresses in place, the girls went to hunt wild animals. Cautiously they crept up to the corral and shot imaginary arrows at Rembrandt.

The next day, they played the Indian game again. This time Eloise decided her doll, Clara, had a fever. Blossom gathered seed pods from under a locust tree. When shaken they made a loud rattling noise. She gave some of the pods to Eloise. Then the girls went to the place where Eloise had laid Clara in the grass.

Blossom, who now spoke Indian, chanted, "Hey, tata chu chum."

Eloise joined in. "Hey, tata chu chum."

Clara said nothing. She just stared at them merrily through blue X eyes.

Both girls shook their rattles and walked slowly in a circle. As they moved, they chanted. Around and around they went, chanting and rattling, until Eloise declared that Clara's fever was cured.

The following day, Eloise no longer wanted to wear a feather in her bonnet. Feathers were for Indian scouts and she now had a more important job to do.

At the foot of the attic stairs was a place where

three pegs had been set into the wall. There her father kept an assortment of broken leather belts, reins and straps. From these she selected a long leather thong. She tied it around Clara's neck and swung Clara on to her back. Then she tied the loose ends around her own neck.

"I'm a squaw now! See, Clara is my papoose."

That afternoon, the girls busied themselves collecting plants and herbs in one of Mrs. VanEyck's pots. When the pot was nearly full, the squaw stirred the plants with a wooden spoon and served a big dinner to the tribe. Clara was very hungry and ate it all.

Finally, Eloise thought up her best Indian game. It took most of the morning to secretly gather the things she needed, but by playtime she was ready.

"Blossom, do you know what today is?" she asked excitedly.

Blossom laughed. "How could I know, Miss Eloise? You just made it up."

"Today is Ceremony Day!" Eloise announced, and from the tone of her voice, Blossom knew Eloise had something very special in mind.

Eloise handed Blossom a sack. "Here, Blossom, you carry this. It's for our ceremony, but we have to go to the top of the Indian Path to have it."

So Blossom took the sack and followed Eloise out of

the yard. They crossed the dirt road and were soon on what Eloise called the Indian Path. It took them to the top of a high hill.

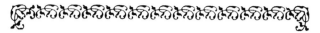

THE CEREMONY

The Indian Path wound so steeply up through the woods that Eloise had to stop and rest for a while before reaching the top. But once there, she walked briskly across a small clearing, then beckoned for Blossom to follow.

The girls were standing on the edge of a high cliff. Far down to their left was the wide Hudson River. In the distance, directly ahead, a cluster of rooftops made up the village of Nyack. West of the village, a mountain ridge worked its way north to the place where they stood, then it turned sharply east toward the river.

"See how the mountain bends out toward the river," Eloise said. "We call this place Verdrietige Hook. That's Dutch! It means long hard work. Sailors named it that because it takes so long to sail by.

Next Eloise pointed directly below. "There! That's where Camboan lives. In the old days, Indians came to this mountain in canoes. They had secret ceremonies here. Just like the one we're going to have."

Then, taking the sack, she yelled "Hey!" and tumbled to the ground.

Blossom settled down beside her. She was curious to see what Eloise had brought. Eloise opened the sack and took out the chicken feather and her papoose. Eloise put the papoose on her back and Blossom put the feather in her hair. When they were ready, Eloise dug into the sack again. This time she took out a piece of charcoal and a tin of white flour.

"We need to paint our faces for the ceremony. Don't you think?"

Blossom clapped her hands in glee.

Eloise dipped her fingers into the flour and then dabbed some on Blossom's face. "We're going to be sisters in the same tribe and sisters have to look alike. So I'm going to make half of your face white. Then you can make half of my face black. That's what the ceremony is all about."

Blossom sat very still, waiting for Eloise to finish. She wished she had brought the broken mirror from her room in the attic. She wanted to see how she looked with a white face.

Finally, Eloise finished spreading the white dust and it was Blossom's turn. She took the charcoal and drew a long line from Eloise's forehead, down her nose to

54

her chin. Then she darkened one side of Eloise's face. It was fun to do.

When both their faces were properly painted, Eloise dug into the sack again. This time, she took out her father's clay pipe.

"Hey! Miss Eloise, I think we're gonna be in big trouble if your papa finds out about this."

"I know, but we have to do it. Indians always smoke pipes when they have ceremonies."

"Are we really going to smoke it?" Blossom asked.

"Hey!" Eloise answered and held up a piece of flint for starting a fire.

Her plan was to build a small fire, then use a stick from the fire to light the pipe. But as it turned out, starting a fire was not easy to do.

They began by gathering small sticks for kindling. Eloise scratched the flint against a stone, but she could not make a spark. Reluctantly, she handed the flint over to Blossom, who struck the flint much harder against the stone. Several sparks flew into the air and landed on the kindling. The girls stared, expecting to see long tongues of flame leap upward. Nothing happened.

Blossom struck the flint against the stone again and again, but no matter how many sparks she made, the sticks would not blaze. Both Blossom and Eloise were disappointed—they would have to pretend.

Eloise carefully positioned the clay pipe on the ground between them and began the ceremony.

"Sisters in the same tribe," she said haltingly.

Then with great dignity she lifted the pipe to her lips. There was a long hollow sucking sound as she drew on the pipestem.

"Hey!" she said and she extended the pipe to Blossom.

"Hey, cho to ta," Blossom said to the half black, half white face opposite her. She raised the pipe to her mouth. It made the sucking sound again. Next, she pretended to cough the way grown men often did when they smoked.

"Strong tobacco," she grumbled.

Neither girl laughed. The ceremony had become too real.

Eloise took the pipe from Blossom and carefully placed it on the ground. She handed Blossom some of the locust pod rattles and said, "Now we'll do the Sister Dance."

They got to their feet, shaking the rattles very slowly and very rhythmically. They circled the clay pipe and chanted, "Sisters in the same tribe. Sisters in the same tribe."

Eloise was turned in such a way that Blossom only

saw a black face below the blue bonnet. Eloise looked oddly more alive. Even Clara looked real as she bobbed up and down on Eloise's back.

As for Eloise, she saw only the white half of Blossom's face. Blossom's dark skin glowed beneath

the faint white dust, and the chicken feather at the back of her head made her look like an Indian princess.

As the chanting went on, the girls moved faster.

Their voices rose louder and louder.

"Sisters in the same tribe." Rattle, rattle. "Sisters in the same tribe." Rattle, rattle. On and on they went, until they were quite dizzy and dropped to the ground.

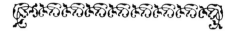

THE CLIFF

Blossom lay patiently waiting for the world to stop spinning. Overhead, three hawks flew in wide lazy circles. She watched as the breeze caught their wings and carried them high in the sky. Once there, the graceful birds circled and glided earthward again.

Eloise's stomach felt empty. She was sorry she hadn't brought something to eat. So leaving Blossom to watch the hawks, she went to hunt for berries.

Blossom closed her eyes and pretended she was one of the big birds. She stretched her arms wide and let the wind carry her over the mountain. Hawks flew all around her and she pretended one of them had blue eyes and yellow feathers. She flew faster. The blue-eyed hawk beat its wings, but Blossom was moving too fast for the blue-eyed hawk to keep up.

When she stopped pretending and opened her eyes, the real hawks were still there, but Eloise was nowhere in sight. The pipe and flour tin were on the ground nearby. She gathered them together and was putting them in the sack when she heard Eloise scream.

Blossom went to the top of the Indian Path and looked down the hill, but Eloise was not there. She walked along the edge of the clearing and peered into the woods. She called Eloise's name several times, but there was no answer. She crossed the clearing to where the path worked its way down to Nyack. She called again. Still there was no answer.

Something near the cliff caught her eye. There, on a berry bush, hung a blue sunbonnet. Blossom neared the cliff edge and peeked over. Clara's happy face smiled up at her from twenty feet below and next to her, on a wide ledge, was Eloise.

"Miss Eloise!" Blossom cried in alarm. "Don't move, Miss Eloise, I'll get you."

But getting there was not going to be easy. Blossom studied the rocky cliff walls, until she spied a place where chunks of stone had torn away leaving lots of tiny footholds. She examined the place once more to be sure it was safe for climbing, then she slipped over the side.

She worked her way downward, carefully planting each foot squarely before releasing her hand grip above. Finally she was on the ledge. She could hear Eloise moving somewhere to the left. So after taking a deep breath, she edged in that direction.

Suddenly there was a loud crack! Blossom looked back to see the ledge breaking apart. Big stones were sliding downward. They thumped and crashed against the rocky cliff, then disappeared below.

A shiver ran up her spine. A moment ago she'd been standing right there. Now that part of the ledge was gone. Eloise was close by, extending her hand. Blossom took a step and let Eloise grab her.

"I've got you, Blossom. I've got you!" Eloise yelled as they wrapped their arms around each other and held one another tight.

Soon Eloise was saying, "I want to go home, Blossom. I want to go home."

Blossom was frightened. Every time she heard Eloise say, "I want to go home," she got more worried. She looked for a way back up to the clearing, but with part of the ledge gone, it was no longer possible to reach the jutting rocks she had climbed down. The corners of Blossom's mouth turned downward and she felt hot tears fill her eyes.

Eloise held Blossom in her arms and tried to quiet her. "Please don't cry, Blossom. We'll get home some-how." Blossom couldn't stop crying. She used the hem of her apron to wipe her eyes, but the tears kept coming.

Eloise wanted to be brave. She wanted to make

Blossom feel better, but being brave was difficult. Her ankle hurt from the fall and she wanted her mother. It was all too much for her to bear. Soon Eloise was crying, too.

The tears that streamed down her cheeks made white streaks in the black charcoal. When Blossom saw them, she wanted to laugh.

"Your ceremony paint is running, Miss Eloise," she managed to say. "You look dumb."

"I'm not dumb. You're dumb," Eloise shot back between sobs. "You're dumb for coming down here. You should have gone for help. Now we're both stuck!"

Blossom lost her temper, and for the first time, she spoke to Eloise without saying "Miss."

"You're the dumb one, Eloise. You're so dumb you fell off a cliff!"

"It was an accident!" Eloise shouted.

"It was a dumb accident and you did it, Eloise."

Eloise was speechless. She didn't like being blamed. It made her so angry she decided never to speak to Blossom again.

Mrs. VanEyck stood at the back door. Her eyes scanned the yard, the barn, then the fields. "Where are they? Blossom knows I need her to help with dinner."

She walked to the well and lowered the bucket. All the while, she kept a lookout for the girls.

Mr. VanEyck mopped his brow. He had been chopping firewood and now he wanted a cool drink. As he approached the well, his wife offered him a dipper of water.

"Jarvis, where can they be?" Mrs. VanEyck asked. "I'm getting worried."

"They're playing and have probably forgotten the time," he answered. But when he looked into his wife's eyes he added, "If you like, I'll go look in the barn. Sometimes I catch them in there jumping in the hay."

Mr. VanEyck walked a few paces, then called over his shoulder, "Maria, do I smell something burning?"

Mrs. VanEyck grabbed the water bucket and rushed back to the house.

Later Mr. and Mrs. VanEyck ate burned venison in silence. Neither Eloise nor Blossom had returned and both parents were on edge.

Mr. VanEyck didn't think the girls were at the lake. Eloise had promised not to go there again and it wasn't like Eloise to disobey her mother. What bothered Mr. VanEyck was the new rumor he'd heard about a warship out in the river. If English soldiers had landed in the area, not even little children were safe.

64

So while it was still daylight, Eloise's parents left their dinner and went to look for their daughter. They called and shouted, "Eloise," many times, but no one answered.

It was getting very dark on the cliff. The girls pressed their backs against the rocky wall and stretched their legs out in front of them.

Eloise had stopped being angry. She still thought it was wrong of Blossom to have called her "dumb." After all, she hadn't fallen over the edge on purpose. It was an accident and anybody could have an accident.

Still, she was glad Blossom had climbed down to help her. How could Blossom have known the stupid ledge would break? She was glad they'd had the Indian ceremony. Eloise had never had a real sister and it made her feel safer to have one now.

"I'm glad you're here, Blossom. I'd be awfully scared by myself."

"Me too. I'm scared, too," Blossom answered, and she was scared. She was scared a wild animal would come and eat them. She didn't know how a wild animal could get down on the ledge, but it worried her anyway. Perhaps it would be a dumb animal and it would fall over the cliff the way Eloise did.

There was that word "dumb" again. "Well," she thought, "it was dumb. Dumb, dumb, dumb, dumb, dumb!" Then, in another moment she thought, "Eloise couldn't have known the ledge would break. If only the ledge hadn't broken, everything would be all right."

"Eloise, do you think anyone will find us here in the dark?" she asked.

"I know my father will look for us. He may not be able to see us here, but maybe if we're real quiet, we'll hear him calling."

So as night came, the girls listened.

At daybreak, Mr. and Mrs. VanEyck were in the parlor. Neither had been able to sleep. Mrs. VanEyck had busied herself sewing while Mr. VanEyck read the Bible. Now they prepared to search for the children.

Mrs. VanEyck promised to look near the lake. Mr. VanEyck saddled his horse and went to question the neighbors.

During the night Eloise had wedged Clara against the rock wall and used her as a pillow. Blossom had fallen asleep with her head resting on Eloise's shoulder. When they awoke it was daylight.

"What are you thinking, Blossom?"

"I was thinking about the chickens. If we were home, I'd be feeding the chickens right now."

"If we were home," Eloise said, "you could get us some eggs. I wish I had an egg. I'm awful hungry."

Blossom was hungry, too. She thought if she were home, she'd not eat one but two eggs. Then she'd drink a gallon of buttermilk. She was very thirsty.

Eloise rolled down her stocking and rubbed her ankle. "It looks all right," she said, "but it still hurts."

Blossom wasn't interested in Eloise's ankle. She had spotted the hawks. They were high over the mountain. Blossom saw one of the hawks suddenly dive out of the sky. It flew straight for the ledge.

Eloise saw it, too. As the hawk got closer, she hid her face in her hands.

Blossom's heart was pounding. The bird was coming right at her. Its black eye was fixed on hers.

She saw the great bird swerve. It flew out away from the cliff and disappeared.

Blossom leaned forward and peeked over the edge. The hawk was a few feet away, flying close to a narrow ledge.

Blossom watched it glide along the ledge far in the direction of the river. Then it soared back over the mountain and joined its friends.

"Look, Eloise!" Blossom yelled, but Eloise had her hands over her eyes and wouldn't take them away.

Blossom looked again. She saw that the ledge below was much narrower than the one they were on, but she was sure they could stand on it.

"Eloise! Eloise, stop hiding. Look down there. I see another ledge. If we can get to it, maybe we can find a way back up."

Eloise took her hands from her eyes and looked around. "Where did it go?" she asked.

"What go? Oh, the hawk. It's gone. Look down there."

Eloise shook her head. "No! It makes me dizzy to look down," she insisted. "Nothing in the whole world can make me look down there."

"Eloise, sometimes you're so du...." But Blossom held her tongue. There was no use fighting.

Eloise felt worse now than ever. Maybe Blossom was right. Maybe they could find a way off the cliff. She wanted to try, but it scared her to be up so high. No, she couldn't do it. She had to stay where she was and wait for her father to find them.

Mr. VanEyck had ridden from farm to farm questioning each neighbor about the girls. No one had seen them and he was sick from worry.

He looked at the heavily wooded countryside. If Eloise had only told her mother where she was headed, he would know where to begin his search. But who could know?

Then it came to him. There was one neighbor who might be able to help—one neighbor he hadn't yet spoken to. That neighbor lived on the other side of the mountain. To get there, he would have to use the Indian Path through the woods.

The sun beat down on the ledge. Eloise could feel her face and arms burning. She was thirsty and she was hungry. Worst of all, she was beginning to give up hope.

Blossom was on her stomach, looking over the edge. She pointed down to the narrow ledge and said, "See, it's not too far. I can get there. You stay here, Eloise. I'll try to find a way back to the top. Then I'll go get help."

Eloise grabbed Blossom's hand. "No, Blossom. We're sisters now and we have to stay together. I'll go with you."

Blossom gave Eloise a broad smile. "Hey!" she

shouted. "Here we go!"

So while Blossom dangled her legs over the ledge, Eloise fixed Clara to her back. Then when Blossom was safely on the lower ledge, it was Eloise's turn.

She lay on the edge and slowly stretched her feet downward. She felt herself straining to hold on. She wished she'd stayed safely where she was.

"It's only another couple of inches," Blossom coaxed. "Just let go, Eloise, you'll be all right."

Eloise closed her eyes and let herself drop. Now on the narrower ledge, she looked over the side. Quickly she turned her face to the rocky wall. "Oh, it's awfully high," she whined.

Blossom led the way, and the girls inched slowly sideways along the cliff. With each step they moved farther away from the clearing, the Indian Path and home.

Mr. VanEyck came to the top of the path. He trotted the horse across the clearing and began working his way down the hill toward Nyack. Had he been there a little sooner, he might have looked at the cliffside and seen his daughter. But by the time he got there, the girls had already worked their way far from his view.

STRANGERS

By midday Blossom and Eloise were high over the river. A cool breeze blew up from the water, but it dried Blossom's face until she thought her cheeks would crack. She was hungry and very thirsty. Her hands bled from rubbing them against the cliff and her legs no longer wanted to work. Worst of all, she had begun to think there was no way off the cliff.

She was sorry she hadn't listened to Eloise and stayed where they were, but there was nothing she could do about that now. She had to keep going.

As for Eloise, at first the height scared her. Looking over the edge made her dizzy and she feared she would fall. She wished she could be more like Blossom. To her, Blossom was the bravest girl in the whole world. So after a while, Eloise made up her mind to forget everything that made her afraid. She thought only of Blossom. With Blossom leading, she knew they would get home.

Blossom rounded a curve in the rock wall. Just ahead, she saw a pile of boulders clinging to the cliff-side. Instantly she knew they had found a way to the top. Eloise was close behind her. From the look on her face, it was clear Eloise had seen it, too.

Carefully Blossom stepped forward. "Did someone say something?" she asked herself. She turned to Eloise, but Eloise hadn't spoken.

There it was again—a man's voice.

Blossom looked down. A hundred feet below two men stood talking near the base of the cliff. The taller one was dressed in a bright red jacket. A white wig covered his head and gave him the look of someone important. With him was a rough-looking fellow in woodsman's clothing. Farther away, she saw two more men in red jackets. They carried muskets and guarded a small boat that had been hauled onto the beach.

"Help!" Blossom called, but her mouth and throat were so dry she barely made a sound. She raised her arm and waved.

Eloise caught her hand. "No," she croaked hoarsely. "They're British soldiers. They'll kill us."

"They'll help us," Blossom insisted.

Eloise shook her head. "Red uniforms," she whispered. "They're soldiers. Don't wave to them."

Blossom had never seen British soldiers, but she'd

heard lots of terrible things about them and she'd heard about their red coats. "Maybe Eloise is right," she thought. "I wish I knew what to do."

The men were speaking again, and the wind carried their voices up the rocky cliff so that the girls heard every word.

The one with the wig said, "When I see your lantern, I'll send twelve men ashore. Is that enough to get the job done?"

The woodsman laughed, "Aye, Captain, they're only simple farmers—no match for your soldiers."

Blossom's heart sank. Eloise was right. The men were soldiers—soldiers who could aim their muskets up at the cliff. She looked quickly around, but there was nowhere to hide.

"How far is it to this place where we land?" the captain asked.

"Two miles to the north and well hidden by the cliffs," came the answer. "With your Lordship's permission, I say we drive the cattle back to the landing and slaughter them there. There's other captains have used that very spot."

Just then, the woodsman turned so that the girls could see his face. A long red scar ran down his cheek. One eye was partially closed and the corner of his mouth sagged cruelly.

The crooked mouth went on. "When you come ashore, you'll see there's a break in the cliff where I can lead you to the top. Then it's through the woods to the Lake Road. Another two miles and we'll hit the first farm. We'll have their stock and be back to the landing before they know what's happened."

"There'd better be no foul-ups. Are you sure you can find your way in the dark?" the captain asked with an angry tone.

"There'll be a full moon, Captain. Trust me, I know these parts like I know my own hand."

"Trust? I don't trust you at all, Smith," the captain snapped. "If one man of the *Vulture's* crew is lost, I'll personally carve up the rest of your ugly face with my sword."

"Now, now, Captain!" the man with the scar stammered. "Old Smith's the King's loyal subject. Every word I say is the truth as you'll see tomorrow night."

The speakers moved off to where the others guarded the rowboat. They pointed to something in the river, but the girls could no longer hear what was said. They watched as the three red-coated soldiers stepped into the boat. The captain settled himself in the prow while the other two took up the oars.

The man with the scar watched until the rowboat was well out in the river. Then he turned and disappeared around a bend in the shoreline.

Staring wide-eyed, Eloise was pressed against the cliff. Blossom tugged at her sleeve. She saw Eloise blink like someone waking from a bad dream. Blossom pointed to the boulders and the girls began edging their way forward again.

Finally they were climbing up the cliff. Blossom could hear Eloise struggling behind her, but she didn't look back until she reached the top. Then she saw that Eloise had gotten her foot wedged in the rocks—the same foot she'd injured in the fall.

Eloise pulled at her foot and felt a sharp pain spread through her ankle. She wanted to cry, but she knew her brave Indian sister wouldn't hear. She pulled at the foot again. This time, her foot slipped out of its shoe and she was free. Blossom reached out her hand for Eloise to grab. In a moment both girls were safely off the cliff.

At first they rested. Then they looked around and discovered the top of the mountain was thick with trees. Neither Blossom nor Eloise knew which way led toward home. For the next few hours they wandered around aimlessly. They tore their dresses on sharp thorns. They tripped over hidden roots. But no matter which way they turned, they could not find a way out of the woods.

Day was quickly turning to night when the girls collapsed in a pile of dead leaves. Birds and small animals made strange rustling sounds not far off, but they were too exhausted to care.

Blossom closed her eyes. The woods were very large and she felt very small. She had tried her best to get them home, but she was only a little girl.

She opened her eyes and peered into the shadows. Something was there. She looked harder, trying to make sense out of what she saw. Was it a bird? Yes, she clearly saw three white-tipped feathers hovering over her. No! It was a man. It was the Indian, Camboan.

"Hey!" she whispered, wishing she knew more Indian words. She wanted to tell him they needed help.

Camboan's hand gently lifted her head and she felt a flask touch her lips. For the first time in over a day, Blossom tasted water.

"Not too much, child," she heard him say in perfect English.

Just then Eloise moaned and Camboan moved to her side. As he held the flask for her to drink, he said, "You must be the one called Eloise. Your father asked me to find you."

"Oh, please take us home. Please!" Eloise begged. "We want to go home. I want to see my father and my mother."

"Yes, yes, I promise. I'll take you there, but not now. It's getting too dark to travel safely through the forest. We'll wait 'til morning."

Over his shoulder he carried a leather pouch. He reached inside and gave each girl sourdough biscuits, cheese and carrots. While they ate he gathered bits of dried leaves, grass and sticks. They watched him strike a flint against a stone. Sparks flew and landed on one of the leaves. Camboan bent closer and gently blew at the leaf until it glowed. He added a single blade of dry grass, then another. Tiny flames soon danced in the darkness. He added small sticks—as each flared he added a larger one until finally he had a comfortable fire.

All the while, Blossom studied him carefully. "We tried to make a fire but we couldn't do it," she said, remembering the clay pipe they'd left behind.

"Starting a fire isn't easy," he said. "My grandfather taught me how. He said fire is a powerful spirit that does not like to be wakened. You must coax the fire to life."

Eloise filled her mouth with biscuits and cheese, and while she chewed, she rolled down her stocking and felt her ankle. When Camboan saw how swollen it was, he leaned closer. Carefully he moved her foot from side to side.

78

"You won't walk far on that, but it's not broken," he said. Then using his knife, he cut a strip from her petticoat and wrapped the ankle tightly.

Blossom watched the fire's light flickering on Camboan's deeply lined face. He looked very wise and much older than she'd noticed before. She wondered why he shaved part of his hair and why he wore three feathers in it. Whatever the reasons, she thought Mr. VanEyck was right. They were safe with him.

When he'd finished wrapping Eloise's foot, he said, "There, that should feel better. Now, Eloise, tell me your friend's name."

"She's Blossom," Eloise answered.

"Blossom," he repeated. "My grandfather would have liked that name." Then with a grin, he added, "But Grandfather might have called her Little Chicken Woman."

Blossom looked at Eloise. Eloise looked at Blossom.

Blossom put her hand to her hair. She couldn't believe it—the chicken feather was still there.

"Oh, I don't know how that got there," she lied as she wrestled the feather out of her hair.

Eloise let out a giggle with her mouth full of cheese. It was the first time all day that either of them had laughed.

Blossom felt too embarrassed to laugh. She wondered if Camboan knew they had been playing Indians.

Camboan went on speaking. "I found a bonnet and saw where one of you fell from the cliff. I guessed the other climbed down to help, but why didn't you girls stay where you were?" he asked.

"We waited all night, but no one came," Eloise explained. "Then this hawk flew at us and scared us."

"No," Blossom interrupted. "It didn't scare me. It showed me the other ledge, the one we used to get to the top."

"Are you sure it was a hawk?" Camboan asked with real interest.

"Oh, yes," Eloise insisted. "It was a hawk. A big hawk."

"Blossom, you said it showed you the other ledge. How did it show you?" Camboan asked.

"It flew toward us, but I think it was looking only at me," Blossom explained. "Then it dove and flew along the lower ledge. That's when I knew we could get to the top."

Camboan grew silent, but he looked at Blossom in such an odd way that she began to feel uncomfortable. She wished he'd stop studying her, so after a minute,

Blossom asked, "Mr. Camboan, where are the other Indians? How come you're the only one who lives here?"

Camboan turned toward the flames dancing in the fire. When he answered there was magic in his voice.

"In the time of my father, my people lived where the great river was wide. Fishing and hunting were good. Our women built great longhouses. I was a child and practiced with my bow.

"There were white traders then, but not so many. More white people came. They cut down the trees. Their cows ate the grass.

"Soon the animals left the forest and my people went without food. Many in the village became sick. Our sachem said we should take the sick ones in our canoes and leave that place. We came here to the shore below the high cliff. Here we fasted and prayed.

"A great hawk came to our campfire and spoke so that all the people understood. It said the white ones had brought the sickness. It said our people could not be cured.

"The people asked the hawk to ease their suffering. The great hawk spread its wings until a shadow fell over the mountain.

"Each one who was sick changed into a bird that flew into the forest. My mother was with them. She was a hummingbird. I tried to catch her and hold her down, but the hummingbird is small and she flew through my fingers.

"Again the hawk spoke. It said its magic would guard the mountain for the Indians. That we should build our longhouses here under its protection. When the hawk had finished speaking it flew to the top of the mountain and circled so that everyone could see.

"But the people were still angry. They took their clubs and went to join the tribes who made war against the whites. Only I stayed. This is where the spirits of my people are. I hear them singing in the forest. Soon I will join them. Until then, I wear the hawk feather to catch the hawk's spirit in the air. I am guided by it's wisdom."

When Camboan finished speaking the fire was low, but Blossom could see the sadness in his face. Eloise was sleeping soundly with Clara in her arms. Blossom stretched out and closed her eyes.

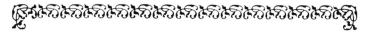

THE HOMECOMING

The next morning, Mr. and Mrs. VanEyck looked out the window to see Camboan entering the yard with Blossom beside him. Her dress was torn and her dirty face was spotted with a strange white dust. And there, riding on Camboan's back, was their daughter. Poor Eloise! Her matted blond hair was covered with bits of dry grass and her sunburned face was smudged with charcoal.

"Eloise, oh, Eloise," Mrs. VanEyck screamed as she and her husband ran from the house.

Mrs. VanEyck took Eloise into her arms and kissed her. Mr. VanEyck called her his pet and stroked her blond hair. The family was whole again, and in their excitement they hugged, laughed and cried all at the same time. Off to the side, Blossom and Camboan stood quietly watching.

Finally Mrs. VanEyck noticed Eloise's bandaged ankle and carried her into the house. Mr. VanEyck remained outside. He had something he wanted to say to Camboan.

"All night I prayed that God would send you to them in time. Now I'm grateful to Him and to you, old friend."

"I too prayed," Camboan said. "I asked the Hawk Spirit to help me pick up their trail and the spirit answered."

Mr. VanEyck didn't believe in hawk spirits, but that didn't matter. He respected his friend. "You must thank the Hawk Spirit for me," he said.

All this time, Blossom had waited for someone to notice her. Finally Mr. VanEyck took hold of her hand. "You poor child," he said. "What a terrible time you've had. Come inside. Your mistress and I want to take care of you."

They were about to enter the house when the aged Indian took a feather from his braid and placed it in Blossom's hair.

"I've never given a hawk feather to anyone before, Blossom, but I think you're the right person to have this one."

Blossom reached up and felt the long feather. She wasn't sure why Camboan had chosen to give it to her, but it was the nicest gift she'd ever been given. She waved to him as he left the yard, then she and Mr. VanEyck went into the house.

Mrs. VanEyck was putting the finishing touches on a

84

new bandage for Eloise's ankle. While she worked, Eloise told all about the cliff. Naturally her parents had lots of questions, and while the girls answered them, Mrs. VanEyck filled two bowls with hot soup. That's when Eloise remembered something important.

"We saw British soldiers! They were near the river, but we heard them. They're going to come here tonight. They're going to rob us."

"Yes, Master VanEyck, there were four men. Three were in red coats and one had a big scar like this," Blossom said as she pulled on her face.

Mr. VanEyck almost laughed at the comic Blossom, but British soldiers were not a laughing matter. He and Mrs. VanEyck made the girls tell exactly what they had seen and heard. When they were finished, the mood in the kitchen had changed.

Mrs. VanEyck took hold of her husband's hand. "Jarvis, I'm frightened. If the children are right, we're in great danger."

"Be calm, dear. You're safe for now. I'll ride to warn the neighbors and get back here before dark."

Mr. VanEyck took his musket with him when he left the house. Mrs. VanEyck watched him leave, then bolted the door.

Jarvis VanEyck found his neighbor piling rocks on to a low rock wall that rimmed his flax field. When he explained all that had happened, Garret Blauvelt was doubtful.

"Jarvis, we can't get armed men together based on a story told by children. They were probably so frightened they didn't know what they saw. And did you stop to think, maybe they made it all up so you won't punish them? Children are apt to do such things."

"They both tell the same story, Garret, and I believe them. Besides, my Eloise has never lied before."

Garret Blauvelt wasn't convinced. "Just think, Jarvis. If those children were on the cliff, how could they hear what was said so far away?"

Mr. VanEyck knew it was strange, but sometimes sound played funny tricks, especially along those cliffs. "Perhaps it was an echo," he suggested.

Just then, something else the girls had said crossed his mind. "Garret, the girls said the men called the ship the *Vulture*. How could they know that? They never heard it from me."

Mr. Blauvelt stroked his brown beard. "They said one of the men had a scar? Hmmm! During the raid at Haverstraw, one of our lads fought with a woodsman. The lad used a knife and it's just possible..."

"It must be the same man," Mr. VanEyck interrupted. "They'll anchor somewhere below Verdrietige where the ship can't be seen. Then they'll send men ashore to steal our cattle. They need food for their army. Don't you see? The girls couldn't possibly have made all of this up."

"Hold on!" Garret Blauvelt said cautiously. "If the girls are right, the raid may be on the Snedecker farm to the north. We don't have enough men to patrol the whole countryside."

So the two men decided on a plan. Garret Blauvelt would alert all the local families. Jarvis VanEyck would go to the top of the Indian Path and prepare a large bonfire. The Snedeckers would prepare a similar fire to the north. If anything happened during the night, someone would light one of the fires. That would be the signal for the militia to come and help.

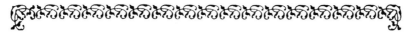

THIEVES IN THE NIGHT

After dark, they all gathered in the parlor with their heads bowed while Mr. VanEyck prayed.

"Lord, watch over us this night. Strengthen our faith to do your bidding and protect us from an evil government. Amen." He looked somber but calm.

"Maria," he said, "I want you to bolt the door and keep the candles unlit. The children should best sleep in the attic where they'll be out of the way. I'll keep watch outside the house. From there, I'll have a good view of the road. If I see anyone, I'll have plenty of time to get to the top of the hill, set the bonfire and be back before they arrive."

The girls went up to the attic, but they didn't try to sleep. They were too excited for that. They sat by the window and peered through the darkness in the direction of the lake.

It was hours before Blossom saw a tiny flash of moonlight against shiny metal. She pressed her nose against the windowpane and waited to see it again. This time Eloise saw it, too.

"Blossom, did you see that?" Eloise wanted to know.

"Uh-huh! There's surely something moving down there," Blossom said in a hushed tone. "Miss Eloise, I'm scared."

"Me too," Eloise whispered, "but don't worry. Father is down there and he saw it too. He'll go set the fire and bring help. My father won't let anything happen to us."

Mr. VanEyck had taken up his sentry position in the darkness below the attic window, but he could not see over the treetops as the girls had done.

Rembrandt was asleep in the corral when a rat slipped under the fence and began scratching in the hay. The noisy creature startled the calf so that she jumped to her feet. The poor rat scampered off under the fence, but Rembrandt was afraid that the rat would be back. She wanted to be with her mother, Bossie, in the barn.

The nervous little calf sniffed the air. She sniffed again. Yes, her friend Mr. VanEyck was nearby and if she climbed through the fence she knew he would save her.

90

The man with the scar paused in the moonlight. Behind him came a dozen red-coated soldiers with muskets. He spoke softly to one of them. "There's your first farm, Capt'n, and not a candle burning. They're tucked in their beds just as I knew they would be."

"Well done, Smith," the captain said. Then he turned to one of his men. "Pass the word. No shooting! We don't want any sounds alerting the neighbors, but if anyone tries to stop us...." He moved his hand to his collar and gestured with his finger as if it were a knife cutting across a throat.

Mr. VanEyck had still seen nothing, but now he heard voices. He looked across the open yard to the road. "Blast them!" he thought. "They must be very close at hand."

He had to get to the signal fire, but now it would be difficult to cross the yard without being seen. He got to his feet and dashed for a large oak tree not far from the house. He pressed himself against the trunk and held his breath. Men were entering the yard. They walked silently in columns of two with muskets on their shoulders.

Mr. VanEyck waited for the men to pass on the far

side of the tree. When they were near the barn, he would break for the Indian Path.

The soldiers marched brazenly across the yard. They turned the corner of the house and were almost out of sight when a frightened white calf appeared in

the moonlight. She ran full speed past the soldiers. One of them lunged at her, but Rembrandt ran on.

The captain called, "Let it go. When we get the cow, the calf will follow."

With that, the men continued on toward the barn, but Scarface looked back over his shoulder and saw something that made him pause. Rembrandt had stopped to lick something near the oak tree. "Strange," said Scarface. "Now what would a calf want in that tree?" he asked as he turned back to where Mr. VanEyck was hiding.

Jarvis VanEyck raised his fist. As the man approached, Jarvis leapt forward and struck the ugly face. Scarface went reeling. Seeing this, the other soldiers aimed their muskets.

"No shooting!" yelled the captain.

Scarface recovered and jumped at Mr. VanEyck. The two men were on the ground struggling when the captain got there. He raised his pistol and brought it down on Mr. VanEyck's head.

"We'll take care of him when we've finished our business in his barn," he said.

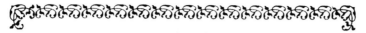

BLOSSOM
AT THE SIGNAL FIRE

Blossom and Eloise were at the window. "They're going to kill my father," Eloise shrieked.

Blossom stared at the unconscious body of Jarvis VanEyck. Her mind raced. "Who will light the signal? Who will stop the soldiers from getting in the house? What will happen to us?"

"We have to do something!" she blurted out loud.

Eloise turned away from the window and looked hard at Blossom. She remembered Blossom on the cliff—how Blossom had found the ledge—how Blossom had led the way. Now she thought, with Blossom at her side, they could do anything.

Calmly Eloise said, "You're right, Blossom. We have to light the signal fire. There's no one else to do it. We have to get help."

Blossom was stunned. This time Eloise was really being dumb. She shook her head. "If we go outside, they'll catch us," she warned.

But Eloise was confident. "We can slip out the back door and get to the woods. We couldn't light a fire the last time, but this time will be different. This time you'll light it, Blossom, I know you will."

With that, Eloise led the way down the narrow staircase to the kitchen. Near the fireplace she found a flint, then she and Blossom slipped silently out the back door.

They heard men's voices down by the barn. So while no one was looking, they ran for the woods.

Once in the woods, the leaves blocked the moonlight. Both girls knew how easy it was to get lost in the woods, but Eloise knew the way. She had played in the woods near her house many times, and in just a few minutes they were on the Indian Path.

"I can't go any farther, Blossom. My ankle is awfully sore. You go ahead, I'll wait here," Eloise said as she handed Blossom the flint.

Blossom hesitated. She didn't want to go by herself, but it was the only way. They'd made it this far and with luck, she might be able to light the fire. She put the flint safely in her apron pocket and went on by herself.

When she reached the top of the path, she stopped before entering the clearing. It was very quiet. She could see the pile of logs waiting. Her hand felt inside her pocket for the flint. It was still there and so was something else—the hawk feather. In a moment, she placed the feather in her hair and stepped into the clearing.

"Hello, Mr. Hawk," she said shyly. "I'm Blossom. I know you guard the mountain for Indians, but I'm kind of an Indian, too. Eloise and I are Indian sisters." Her voice grew louder as she went on.

"I sure would like your help. Mr. Camboan says I have to coax a fire into a flame. Could you help me? It's very important."

When she finished speaking she waited, but everything was quiet just as before. She shrugged and turned to the bonfire.

Mr. VanEyck had piled the logs in a way that looked like a tent. At the front of the tent there was a wide space between the logs. She stuck her hands inside and felt around. The center of the tent was filled with leaves and dry brush. Blossom knew she would have to start the fire there.

She took the flint from her pocket and struck it hard against a stone. One, two, three times she struck the flint. Sparks flew out and landed on one of the dry leaves. Patiently she blew at it until the leaf glowed. She added a single blade of dry grass and blew again. A fine flame jumped into life. Quickly she added another blade of grass, then a small twig, just as she'd seen Camboan do. As the fire grew brighter, she added small sticks, one at a time, being careful not to smother the fire. A bright light filled the darkness. Soon the fire reached the logs and red flames leaped upward.

The blazing bonfire lit up the night. Blossom stepped back as the flames twisted high up over her head. She had done it and she wanted to tell Eloise how easy it had been.

She crossed the clearing and was almost on the Indian Path when she heard wings flapping. She looked to the sky, but there was nothing there.

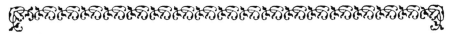

SCARFACE RUNS AWAY

Blossom and Eloise hid in the woods at the bottom of the path. From there, they looked across the road into the yard. The soldiers had seen the signal fire and were hurrying to make their escape. The captain had drawn his sword and waved it over his head. Men were racing across the yard. One of them used a long stick to prod the two cows, Bossie and Matilda, on to the road.

Mr. VanEyck was sitting on the ground beneath the oak tree holding his bloodied head, and Rembrandt was in the flower garden munching. When she saw Bossie leaving the yard, she trotted off to join her.

Scarface was the last to cross the yard. When he reached the oak tree, he stopped and looked down at the half-conscious Jarvis VanEyck.

"Ahh! You're still here and a good thing. I'm going to make you pay for this mess."

The girls watched as Scarface reached inside his

jacket and pulled out a knife. He bent forward and using his left hand, he grabbed Mr. VanEyck by the hair.

At that moment, Rembrandt got tired of walking behind her mother. She paused to rest in the roadway, but the man with the stick was in a hurry. Down came the stick on Rembrandt's back.

No one had ever hit Rembrandt before and she didn't like it. Instead of running ahead to find her mother, she turned around and ran for home.

Blossom and Eloise saw Scarface raise his right hand, the cold steel of his knife flashing in the moonlight. As the knife moved down toward the helpless Jarvis VanEyck, the white calf dashed into the yard with her head low. Rembrandt had never run so hard or so fast before, and by the time she saw Scarface, it was too late to stop. Her head collided with the seat of his pants. Scarface was shoved forward. As he crashed into the tree, the girls heard the metal knife snap.

For a few moments, Scarface lay on the ground stunned. Then he scrambled to his feet and fled.

Later that night, Blossom stood by the fireplace and watched Mrs. VanEyck wrap clean white bandages around her husband's head. Two militiamen, as well as Mr. Blauvelt, were there.

One of the militiamen was speaking. "We chased them to the top of the ridge and down to the landing where their boats were waiting," he said. "We got off a few shots and we wounded two of them. Serves the thieves right."

Garret Blauvelt's deep voice interrupted. "We'll soon be calling that place Slaughter's Landing."

"Aye!" said the militiaman. "That name suits it." Then turning to Mr. VanEyck he went on.

"We've recovered your cattle, Jarvis, except for a white calf that's running wild in the woods. Come daylight, some of the men will find it."

"Thank you for the help and kindness," Mr. VanEyck said, holding his painful head.

The militiaman went on. "During these times, we have to stick together. It's a good thing you got that bonfire going when you did."

Jarvis VanEyck was confused. "But I didn't set the bonfire," he said.

Eloise spoke up. "It was Blossom, Father. Blossom set the fire all by herself," she said.

Everyone in the room turned to look at the little girl with the hawk feather in her curly hair.

"Well, I'll be!" said one of the militiamen.

Blossom said nothing, but her brown face beamed brightly.

Mr. VanEyck slapped his knee loudly. "I wish Old Braun could be here," he said.

"Hush, Jarvis," Mrs. VanEyck scolded. Then she threw her arms around Blossom and hugged her.

If you are interested in acquiring a copy of this book, and it is not available at your local bookstore, please contact the office of the Historical Society of Rockland County, 20 Zukor Road, New City, New York 10956; telephone, 914-634-9629; fax, 914-634-8690. Wholesale and bulk-order discount inquiries are welcomed.